Station Avenue
Elementary School

South Yarmouth, MA 02664

Jafta

Story by Hugh Lewin
Pictures by Lisa Kopper

Carolrhoda Books, Inc. / Minneapolis

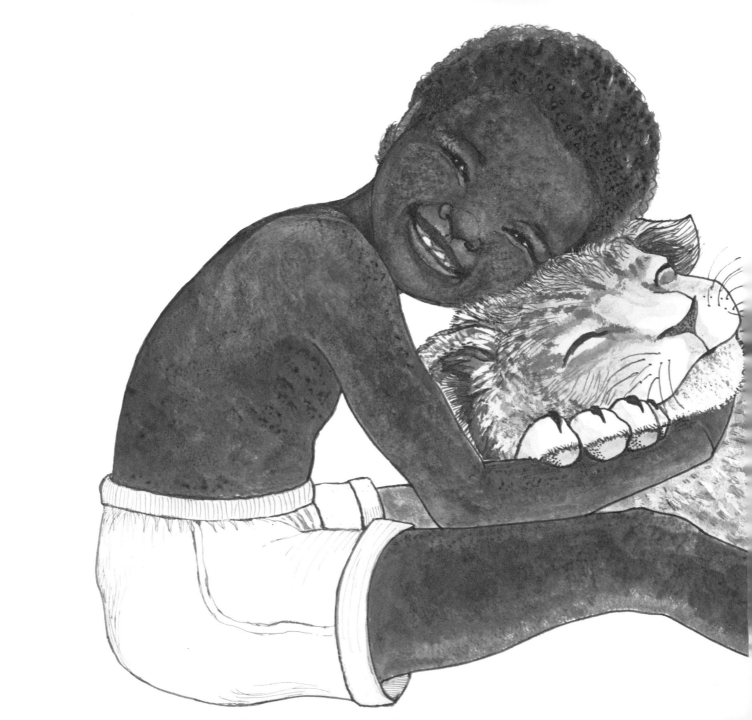

When I'm happy, said Jafta, I purr like a lioncub,

or skip like a spider,

or laugh like a hyena.

And sometimes I want to jump like an impala,

and dance like a zebra,

or just nuzzle like a rabbit.

When I get tired, I like lazing in the sun like a lizard,
or wallowing warm like a hippo,
and feeling cuddly like a lamb.

But when I get cross, I stamp like an elephant
and grumble like a warthog.

(I don't often get cross, said Jafta.)

And I can be as strong as a rhino.

Sometimes I want to be as tall as a giraffe,

as long as a snake.

And I want to run as fast as a cheetah,
as quick as an ostrich,

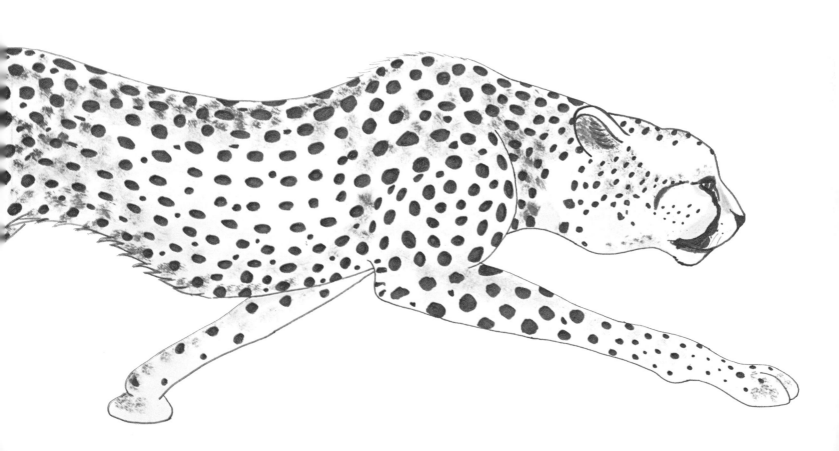

or swing through the trees like a monkey,
and fly high high high like an eagle,

or just stand very still, like a crane on one leg.

But actually, said Jafta,
I don't think there's anything quite so nice

as being a flamingo flying off into the sunset ...

This book is available in two editions:
Library binding by Carolrhoda Books, Inc.
Soft cover by First Avenue Editions
241 First Avenue North
Minneapolis, Minnesota 55401

LIBRARY OF CONGRESS CATALOGING-IN-PUBLICATION DATA

Lewin, Hugh.
  Jafta.

  Summary: Jafta describes some of his everyday feelings
by comparing his actions to those of various African
animals. [1. Animals-Fiction. 2. Africa-Fiction. 3. Emotions-
Fiction] I. Kopper, Lisa, ill. II. Title.
PZ7.L58418Jaf 1983   [E]   82-12847
ISBN 0-87614-207-2 (lib. bdg.)
ISBN 0-87614-494-6 (pbk.)

This edition first published in 1983 by Carolrhoda Books, Inc.
Original edition published in 1981 by Evans Brothers Limited,
London, England.
Text copyright © 1981 by Hugh Lewin.
Illustrations copyright © 1981 by Lisa Kopper.
All rights reserved.

Manufactured in the United States of America